HORSELAND

HarperCollins®, ☙®, and HarperEntertainment™ are trademarks of HarperCollins Publishers.

Horseland #2: Back in the Saddle Again
Copyright © 2007 DIC Entertainment Corp.
Horseland property™ Horseland LCC
Printed in the United States of America.
For information address HarperCollins Children's Books, a division of HarperCollins Publishers,
1350 Avenue of the Americas, New York, NY 10019.
www.harpercollinschildrens.com
www.horseland.com

Library of Congress catalog card number: 2007924693
ISBN 978-0-06-134168-7

Book design by Sean Boggs
❖
First Edition

Back in the Saddle Again

Adapted by
ANNIE AUERBACH

Based on the episode
"BACK IN THE SADDLE AGAIN"

Written by
JOHN LOY

≣HarperEntertainment
An Imprint of HarperCollins Publishers

CHAPTER 1

It's a clear day as Shep walks around the stable. The Australian herding dog loves being at Horseland Ranch.

For humans, it is the perfect place to board, groom, and train a horse. It is also a great place to make friends and have incredible adventures.

For horses, it's a place to be well cared for and form wonderful bonds with their riders. It is also the ideal place to talk about what's happening—for at Horseland, all the animals can talk to one another without the humans having any clue.

For Shep, the ranch is home. His job is to keep the horses in line, and they respect him, even if they don't always agree with him. With seven horses—and seven different personalities—there's never a dull moment.

"At Horseland, there's *always* something going on," Shep says to Angora, as he turns the corner of the stable and sees the fluffy, gray cat sitting on top of a few bales of hay.

Angora yawns and stretches. "Yeah," she

replies sourly. "So much activity, a cat can't even take a nap in peace." She jumps down and joins Shep.

Shep looks over at Angora and just smiles. He knows she can be moody. "Lighten up, Angora," he says. "It's beautiful outside."

As they start to walk away, Angora stops in front of a large mud puddle.

"What's so beautiful about a big mud puddle right in my way?" Angora asks in an annoyed tone.

"So go through it," suggests Shep.

Angora looks horrified. "You've got to be kidding!" she exclaims. She isn't about to get herself all wet and filthy.

"It's just a little mud. Come on, 'fraidy cat," teases Shep. "Give it a try!"

Angora narrows her eyes. She loves a challenge and she's ready to take this one on. "Think I can't? Watch this!" Then she rears back and with perfect catlike grace leaps right over the mud puddle. "Ha! Showed

3

you!" she calls to Shep, as she continues on her way.

Shep smiles to himself just as Teeny the pig walks up.

"Hi, Shep," says the pig. "Nice day, isn't it?" Then she looks down at the mud puddle. "Ew. That looks messy."

"It's just mud, Teeny," says Shep. "What are you afraid of?"

"I'm not afraid of mud," Teeny replies. "I just don't like it much." She shakes her head. "Nope. Not my kind of thing."

Teeny is quite an unusual pig—she doesn't like to get dirty! So the resourceful pig nudges a plank of wood and lays it across the mud puddle, creating a bridge.

Shep laughs at Teeny's creative solution. With her pink-ribboned tail bouncing, Teeny trots across the plank as the dog beside her plows right through the mud puddle.

When they reach the other side, Shep says, "There's nothing wrong with having fears. Everyone faces challenges at some point in their life. It's how you handle them that counts." Shep thinks back to a few days earlier. "Reminds me of when Molly had to face her fears. . . ."

CHAPTER 2

"You got it, Molly?" asked Sarah. "Yeah, almost there," replied Molly, as she placed the pole in the X-shaped stand piece. The girls were helping to set up fences and other obstacles in the arena for a practice jumping session.

Sarah Whitney and Molly Washington were two of the girls who trained and kept horses at Horseland. Their backgrounds couldn't be more different—Sarah was from

6

a wealthy family and Molly's family was more middle class. But the two girls didn't care where they came from. Their love of horses had made them friends.

In another part of the arena, Alma Rodriguez and Bailey Handler were busy setting up poles on either side of a hedge. Four poles needed to be put into position on each side of the shrubbery.

"Got it," said Alma, as she placed the final pole into a post on one side.

Bailey placed his final pole on the other side of the hedge. He wiped his forehead. Even though his parents owned Horseland, Bailey had to do his fair share of the chores. Luckily, he got to ride his horse often enough to make all the hard work worth it.

"There's still one more fence we have to get," Bailey said. He turned and noticed two girls sitting on the sidelines, not lifting a finger to help. "Typical. Chloe and Zoey are sitting it out during all the hard work."

Chloe and Zoey Stilton were extremely

rich, spoiled sisters who considered themselves above everyone else. The idea that they would ever actually *help* the others was inconceivable to them.

Alma looked over at Chloe and Zoey and then rolled her eyes. She wasn't surprised at all. Although she had learned the value of hard work from her father, who was the manager at Horseland, Alma knew that Chloe and Zoey would never offer to help.

In the middle of the arena, Will Taggert surveyed the progress. The oldest of the riders at fourteen, he had the most experience and was in charge. He was going to be teaching the jumping lesson that day.

"The jumps are almost ready," he announced to the group.

Everyone smiled. They couldn't wait to begin the lesson. After all, there was a competition just days away!

Sitting in the shade of a big tree, Shep, Angora, and Teeny watched all the activity going on in the arena.

"What's up, Shep? What's all the commotion?" asked Teeny. The high-strung pig ran in circles. "The place is really jumping today!"

Shep looked at the excited pig and smiled. "You think it's jumping now, just wait until later. The kids are getting ready for a jumping competition," he explained.

Angora got a devilish look in her eyes. "If they're not careful, it's going to be a *falling* competition," she said and snickered. She loved a good drama.

Shep shook his head. "Angora! Don't be so catty," he scolded.

Angora shot him a snide look. "Listen, you know it and I know it: Where there's jumping, there's falling."

Inside, Sarah and Bailey were dragging the final obstacle out of the stable and toward the arena. All of the horses were in stalls that

9

faced each other. The animals were keyed up as they watched Sarah and Bailey. Once the humans left, the horses talked excitedly.

"I love jumping competitions!" exclaimed Aztec with a glint in his eyes. The Kiger mustang was Bailey's horse, and just like Bailey, he loved to take risks. "Going over those hurdles, feeling the wind in your mane—it's a real rush! I can't wait!" He whinnied and vigorously tossed back his brown mane.

"Don't get too carried away, Aztec," said Chili from his stall. The gray Dutch Warmblood stallion belonged to Chloe. Just like his owner, Chili could be arrogant and spiteful. "If anybody here is going to win the competition, it'll be me," he declared.

Across the way, Alma's skewbald pinto mare named Button looked at Calypso in the next stall over. "Nothing's wrong with Chili's self-confidence," Button said to Calypso.

They both knew how full of himself Chili could be. Then a worried look crossed Calypso's face. "I wish I could say the same for Molly," said the spotted Appaloosa mare. "We haven't done much jumping together. I think she may be afraid . . . and that frightens *me*."

"Oh, Calypso, she'll do fine," Button said reassuringly. "Right, Scarlet?"

Button glanced over at Scarlet, who responded with a nod of her head before turning away from the others. The black Arabian mare moaned quietly in pain.

"Oh, I just hope I don't let down Sarah," Scarlet said to herself, shaking her head with worry.

Button and Calypso shared a look. What was wrong with Scarlet . . . and why was she keeping it a secret?

CHAPTER 3

When the jumps in the arena were finally set up, the riders eagerly headed to the stable to get their horses.

"Who wants to go first?" asked Bailey.

"Not me," said Molly.

"I'll go," volunteered Alma.

Everyone entered the stable and went up to his or her own horse. The horses were happy to see their riders.

"Hey, Scarlet!" Sarah called to her horse, as she approached her stall. "How's my girl? Ready to do some jumping?" she asked, as she rubbed the horse affectionately on the nose.

Scarlet did her best to hide the worry in her eyes as Sarah led her out of the stall and toward the arena.

Before long, the group was wearing their riding helmets and mounted on their horses. They lined up at one end of the arena. Will was sitting astride his horse, Jimber, a palomino stallion with black streaks in his golden mane and tail. He and Jimber walked back and forth, explaining the afternoon's lesson.

"Listen up, everyone," began Will. "These are all the different types of obstacles you'll be asked to jump at the competition." He walked by each obstacle as he pointed them out to the group. "We've got a gate, a fence, some parallel bars, and an oxer, which is a combination of a hedge and railing."

Molly gave Will a mischievous smile. "Uh, in case you've forgotten, we helped set them up!" she said.

Everyone laughed, including Will. He gave Molly a good-natured smile as he walked Jimber back to face the others.

"And you did a fine job," Will said with a thumbs-up. "Now, let's learn how to jump over them." Will looked at his cousin Bailey and said, "Why don't you go first?"

Bailey's eyes grew wide, and a smile formed on his face. He and Aztec loved to jump, and they were more than ready to go first.

"Way to go, Bailey," Sarah said encouragingly.

Bailey nudged Aztec forward, and they joined Will and Jimber.

Will gestured to the lowest of the obstacles. "Let's see you jump Aztec over this low fence here," he said.

Bailey nodded and looked at the fence, concentrating hard. Then he and Aztec cantered toward it. They jumped over the fence gracefully, making it look very easy.

The others clapped and cheered.

"All right, Bailey!" called Sarah.

"Bravo!" cried Alma.

"Nice job, Bailey," Will told him.

Chloe and Zoey politely clapped.

Bailey and Aztec turned around and

returned to the group.

"Chloe, were you watching Bailey?" asked Will.

"Always," replied Chloe. It was no secret that the sisters had a crush on Bailey. Chloe blew him a kiss and giggled with Zoey as Bailey blushed.

"Okay, fine," said Will, trying to steer them back to the lesson at hand. "Now, can you tell me anything about his jumping technique?"

Chloe rested her head on her hand, thinking hard. She replayed Bailey's jump in her head and described it for Will.

"He approached the fence at a canter," she began. She thought back to what his feet were doing and remembered that Bailey's heels went down in the stirrups.

"When it was time to jump, he kept his heels down, and he leaned forward just a little bit and pushed back, so his back matched the angle of Aztec's back," she explained. Then she pictured how successfully he completed the jump. "A flawless jump," she added.

"That was great, Chloe! You're absolutely right," said Will with a wink. He was secretly surprised to get such a descriptive and accurate explanation from Chloe. He was glad she had paid such close attention.

Will looked at the six riders on their horses.

"So, Chloe was watching Bailey," he said to them. "But where was Bailey looking?"

Molly frowned in thought. "Where *was* he looking?" she wondered.

Hmm . . . , thought Sarah. Then, suddenly it came to her. "At the fence!"

Will nodded. "That's right. He looked straight ahead, between Aztec's ears, at the fence and beyond it, to where he wanted to land," he explained.

"Oh . . . ," said the group, understanding the process.

Nearby, Shep, Angora, and Teeny watched. Angora wasn't too impressed with Bailey's jump.

"Big deal," she said. "Even I could jump that!"

"With Bailey on your back?" Shep said teasingly.

Angora glared at him. "That's not the point!" she said.

The three animals watched the jumps for a few more minutes before Angora stretched and said, "Okay, boredom setting in." She looked at Shep and Teeny. "Anyone want to go bat a ball of yarn around?"

Shep shook his head. "No, I want to watch them jump."

"Yeah, me too!" added Teeny, as she used the fence post to scratch an itch.

"Fine, see if I care," said Angora. But she was disappointed the others wanted to stay and watch. She hoped there would be some falling soon, instead of jumping. *Now that would be exciting!* she thought mischievously.

CHAPTER 4

N ow Will wanted to see the other riders jump. "Who wants to go next?" he asked.

Zoey raised her hand. "I'll go. You think *he* did a good job? Wait till you see me!" she said confidently. Her horse, Pepper, was a gray Dutch Warmblood mare with a dark-colored coat and a full mane and tail. She and Zoey took off and easily sailed over the fence.

"Great job," said Will.

"Told you," Zoey replied, flipping her hair over her shoulder.

"Okay, Alma," called Will. "You want to take a turn?"

Alma nodded nervously. "Uh . . . *sí*. Yes. I guess I do."

Molly gave her a thumbs-up for support. "You'll be great!" she told Alma encouragingly.

Alma took a deep breath and steered Button into position. She pressed her heels into the horse's side, and the horse reared back. They started to canter, and Button launched herself over the fence, landing perfectly on the other side.

"Great job, Alma!" cheered Sarah.

"You did it, girlfriend!" added Molly.

"That was the best yet!" said Will, clapping. "You and Button really work well together."

Alma beamed, and Button happily pranced around a bit before rejoining the group.

23

However, one girl was not cheering Alma on.

"The best yet? I don't think so," said Zoey. She and Pepper both snottily stuck their heads in the air.

Chloe leaned over. "Don't worry, Sis. I'll get the family honor back," she said to Zoey. She raised her hand and waved. "Hey, Will! Me next!"

"Go for it," replied Will.

Chloe and Chili moved into position. Chili pawed at the ground, and then they took off at a canter. As they reached the fence, Chili's forelegs left the ground just as they were supposed to. But Chloe glanced downward, just for a second. She gasped nervously . . . and then Chili gasped. They lost their positioning, and Chili's hind hooves clipped the top pole of the fence. The pole fell off and hit the ground with a *clunk*. Chili landed clumsily, and Chloe reined him in as he whinnied.

As Chloe and Chili made their way back to the line of riders, Will put the fallen pole back in position. Then he turned to the group.

"So that was a point deduction right there," he explained. "Anybody know what Chloe did wrong?"

Much to Chloe's surprise, it was her own sister who raised her hand.

"She didn't look straight ahead," said Zoey.

25

Chloe gave her a nasty look. When it came to competing, the fact that they were sisters was not important at all. They each wanted to be number one.

"Zoey's right," said Will, as he got back on Jimber. "When Chloe looked down, she shifted her weight forward, which then moved Chili's weight forward, too." He looked intently at each of the riders. "That's something we *all* need to remember. Jumping is about working together with your horse."

All of the riders nodded.

"Molly, you want to go next?" asked Will.

Molly swallowed hard as she and Calypso walked forward. Molly didn't have a lot of experience with jumps and was worried about completing this one. But she put on a brave face and said to Calypso, "We can do this, girl. We can do it!" It wasn't clear if she was trying to convince Calypso . . . or herself.

Molly and Calypso reached the starting point and then began to canter toward the

fence. Calypso's white mane blew backward as they gained speed. When they got closer, Calypso leaped. But at the top of their arc, Molly lost her balance!

"Aaaaaahhh!!!!" cried Molly. With her arms flailing, she fell from the saddle!

27

Calypso made it safely over the fence and immediately turned around, looking for Molly. She neighed with worry, for she saw Molly lying flat on her back—and she wasn't moving!

"**M**olly!" exclaimed Will, as he climbed down off of Jimber. He and the others had rushed over to where Molly had fallen from her horse. "Are you okay?"

Molly made a soft groan but still was not moving much.

"Guys, don't move her," Will warned. He knew that if she had any broken bones, that would be the worst thing to do.

Sarah jumped off Scarlet and kneeled down on the other side of Molly.

"Molly, are you all right? Speak to us!" Sarah pleaded.

Molly suddenly gasped for air. She began to cough and finally caught her breath. She sat up very slowly.

"I just got the wind knocked out of me," said Molly.

Will and Sarah looked at each other, relieved. They helped Molly to her feet. She was a bit unsteady but seemed to be okay.

"Molly, do you want to try it again?" asked Will, pointing to the fence.

Molly hesitated and then shook her head.

"The others can go," she told him. Then she looked at Sarah. "You and Scarlet haven't tried yet."

Sarah smiled at her friend. "Sure. We'll go," she said. Inside, Sarah was concerned. She wished Molly would try again, but she could also understand how scared she must feel.

Molly took hold of Calypso's reins and led her off to the side as everyone else rode back to the other side of the arena.

As Sarah climbed onto Scarlet, the horse winced in pain.

"You okay, girl?" asked Sarah, as she leaned down to stroke Scarlet's neck.

Scarlet quickly pulled her head back up, pretending that nothing was wrong. Sarah and Scarlet got into position. Sarah focused her attention on what she needed to do to complete a successful jump. She urged Scarlet forward and the horse began to canter. When they got to the fence, they took the jump, making it over with ease. Sarah didn't notice Scarlet's pain on the landing . . . and that was just the way Scarlet wanted it. She didn't want Sarah to know her secret— no matter what.

CHAPTER 6

A few days later, Angora snoozed peacefully in the warm afternoon sun outside the stable. Teeny sat nearby, watching the practice going on in the arena.

"Howdy!" said Shep, as he joined them.

Angora gave a big yawn, slightly annoyed at having been woken up from her catnap.

"I see they're still working on their jumps," said Shep, looking toward the arena.

But he noticed someone was missing. Shep looked around and saw Molly sitting on a bale of hay a few yards away from the arena. She was watching the others practice their jumps. Calypso was tethered to one of the posts of the arena fence, all saddled up with no place to go.

"Two whole days and she won't even get back on Calypso," said Shep sadly. "Saddles her up, but won't get on to ride her."

"But why not?" asked Teeny, confused.

"She's scared, I guess," replied Shep.

"Humans call it 'fear of falling,'" Angora explained, as she stretched her back. "Unlike cats."

"Right," agreed Shep. "I wonder how Calypso's taking it. . . ."

By the fence, Calypso looked at Molly and then back at the arena. It didn't look like they were going to be jumping today, which made Calypso sad. In general, the horse was eager to please. She felt frustrated that there was nothing she could do to help Molly get back in the saddle.

Just then, Sarah tethered Scarlet to the fence and went to talk to Molly. Once Sarah was out of earshot, Calypso said, "It was my fault. I know it was. She got scared, and then I got scared."

Scarlet shook her head. "It wasn't you, Calypso," she told her. "Sometimes your rider falls. You just have to—" She groaned with pain.

Calypso looked at her, concerned. "Scarlet, what's wrong with you?"

"It's nothing," replied Scarlet, looking away. "Really."

But Calypso wasn't convinced.

Sarah took off her helmet and sat down next to Molly on the bale of hay.

"Hey, Sarah," said Molly. "You're looking really good out there. You'll do great in the competition. I just know it."

Sarah smiled appreciatively and turned to her friend. "Molly, you've still got a day to practice. You could—"

Molly jumped to her feet. "I'm not entering! You got that?" she barked at Sarah.

Sarah put up her hands defensively. "Fine. I'm sorry," said Sarah, trying to calm her down.

But it didn't work. Molly just became more upset. "In fact," Molly shouted, "I might never enter a competition ever again!" She burst into tears and ran toward the stable.

Sarah was stunned. That wasn't her intention *at all*! "Molly, I'm sorry!" she called after her. "Molly! I didn't mean—"

It was no use. As Molly ran away, Sarah stood there, feeling awful.

CHAPTER 7

It was a misty morning at Horseland. The riders had woken up early to prepare for the day's big competition. After getting the horses from the stable, they walked them to the large trailer parked outside. That's where it got ugly.

"I'm your big sister!" said Chloe. "My horse should get the best spot!"

Zoey wasn't buying it. "Well, you stole Pepper's best bridle!" she accused her sister.

"Did not!" said Chloe.

"Did too!" insisted Zoey.

"So?" Chloe said, folding her arms. "That's what you get for always hiding the curry comb!"

And on and on it went. . . .

Meanwhile, Shep, Teeny, and Angora were watching the argument from afar.

"Bicker, bicker," said Teeny, shaking her head. "Chloe and Zoey sure love to bicker."

Angora gave a condescending laugh. "Oh, Teeny, arguments are the spice of life!" she said. "If everyone got along, just think how boring it would be."

Shep looked over at her. "Frankly, I'd rather be bored," he said.

Angora simply rolled her eyes. She loved a good fight, and as she settled on the fence post, she couldn't wait to see what would happen next.

Outside the trailer, Bailey and Alma waited with their horses.

Bailey shook his head. "I'm *not* getting in the middle of that," he said. "But if those two don't hurry up, we're all going to be late."

Just then Sarah walked up.

"Take a number, Sarah," Bailey said. He motioned to the inside of the trailer. "The squabble sisters are at it again."

44

Alma looked around. "Where's your beautiful horse, Sarah?"

"Yeah, that's what I wanted to tell you guys," began Sarah. "I'm not going."

Bailey was astonished. "Are you kidding?" he asked. Sarah was one of the best riders, and he couldn't imagine why she wouldn't compete.

Alma was just as puzzled. "You're not going?" she asked.

"Really? Cool!" said two voices. Chloe and Zoey came to the end of the trailer. They didn't bother hiding their happiness that Sarah wasn't planning to compete. Now they each stood a better chance of winning a ribbon.

Alma scowled at the sisters. "Enough, you two," she said. Then she turned back to Sarah. "*Por qué?* Why? You don't feel well?"

Sarah hesitated and looked away, thoughtfully. "No, I just . . ." She decided to be truthful. "I've decided I'm going to get Molly riding again."

"Wow," said Bailey, surprised.

"*Caramba!*" added Alma. "Do you want me to stay, too?"

Sarah thanked her and then said, "That's okay. I think I can handle it."

CHAPTER

8

Inside the stable, Molly was keeping busy. Using a pitchfork, she was cleaning out Calypso's stall.

"I may not be able to ride anymore. But I can still muck out a stall with the best," she said to Calypso. She tossed another big forkful of hay into a red wheelbarrow.

Her horse stood sadly in one corner, upset by what she was hearing. Calypso wished Molly's confidence hadn't been broken.

She wished there was something she could do to help.

Suddenly, they both heard the roar of an engine and looked out as the Horseland trailer drove by.

"Good, they've left," said Molly. "No chance of me going now." She was trying to convince herself she made the right decision, but it wasn't really working. She placed the pitchfork in the wheelbarrow, picked up the handles, and started rolling it out of the stable. From her stall, Calypso sadly watched her go.

At that moment, shadows fell across Molly's path. It was Sarah, and by her side was Scarlet, all saddled up.

"Sarah?" said Molly, very surprised to see her friend. "Why didn't you go to the competition?"

" 'Cause I'd rather go for a ride with you," replied Sarah, walking toward her.

Molly blinked. "Yeah?" she asked, touched by Sarah's offer. But then her fear swelled up again. "Well, it's *not* going to happen," she declared and pushed past Sarah with the wheelbarrow.

Sarah's mouth fell open in surprise. "Molly, wait!" she called and ran after her.

Outside, Sarah caught up with her. "I don't think you should give up so easily," she told Molly.

Molly whirled around. "Have *you* ever fallen off your horse and landed so hard you couldn't breathe?" she said angrily. "It's really scary!"

Sarah put a comforting hand on Molly's shoulder. "I know, but . . . I just think you need to face your fear."

Molly pushed Sarah's hand off of her shoulder.

"Oh yeah? What do you know about it?" Molly challenged. She got right in Sarah's face. "Have you ever been really scared of anything?"

Sarah's expression grew distant. She looked down. "As a matter of fact, I have,"

she said quietly.

Sarah thought back to when she was eight years old. Every day, she would walk to school on friendly streets that were lined with leafy trees and huge houses. It seemed perfect . . . except for one house that had a menacing and frightening dog that had to be as huge as the house he lived in.

Sarah would always be late for school because she was afraid of that dog. As she neared the house, the dog's barking and growling seemed to leap over the tall brick wall that surrounded the property. It terrified Sarah so much that she wouldn't walk past that house—not even on the other side of the street! She always took the long way around, which made her late.

One day, her teacher told her that if she had one more tardy, she'd be in big trouble. Sarah didn't know what to do. She knew that if she kept arriving late, she'd have to take the limo to school. But Sarah hated that idea. She didn't want the other kids to see her get out of a limo and think she was a snob.

So she decided it was time to face her fears.

Sarah told her father all about her fear of the scary dog, and he offered to walk with her to school the next day. But Sarah had him stop before they reached the house with the dog. She wanted to face her fears on her own, although having her father there for support certainly was reassuring.

"It's okay, Sarah, I'm right here if you need me," her father told her.

"Thanks, Dad," replied Sarah. She took a deep breath. "I'm going to do it."

Sarah began to walk toward the house. The solid metal gate rattled wildly as the dog jumped against it, barking loudly and endlessly. Then she got her courage up and climbed up to take a peek over the wall. Boy, was Sarah surprised! The big, vicious dog turned out to be a little, white poodle with an enormous bark! Sarah laughed at her own foolishness. But she was so happy that she had overcome her fears.

Unfortunately, when Sarah finished telling her story, Molly was not impressed. "Great story. I'll remember it the next time I'm scared by a puppy," she said to Sarah. Then Molly picked up the wheelbarrow and began walking away.

Sarah ran up and stopped her. "Look, all I'm saying is . . . you can't overcome your fears if you don't face them." Then she thought for a moment. "How about we just walk our horses in the pasture?" she suggested. "If you don't want to ride, you don't have to."

Molly looked at Sarah and thought about the proposal. Finally she nodded. "Okay," Molly agreed. "But just a walk . . ."

CHAPTER
9

With the majestic mountains far in the distance, the rolling green pasture seemed to stretch out forever. Puffy white clouds hung in the sky above as Molly and Sarah walked through the lush grass with their horses.

"It's pretty out here," Sarah said.

"Uh-huh," Molly agreed.

Sarah looked over at her friend. "So . . . ready to give it a try?"

Calypso looked hopeful. Was Molly finally ready to ride again?

Molly hesitated and then shook her head. "Not yet," she replied.

"Really?" asked Sarah, bringing Scarlet to a stop. "We've been walking for a long time. Don't you want to ride for a while? It's easy, remember?" She put her foot in the horse's stirrup and settled in Scarlet's saddle.

Just then, Scarlet shuddered in pain.

"What is it, girl?" asked Sarah, suddenly concerned. She immediately got down from the saddle. "What hurts?"

Sarah rubbed her hands over Scarlet's flank. As she rubbed the side of the horse's belly, Scarlet neighed in pain. Sarah put her ear next to Scarlet's side and listened closely.

When she didn't hear anything, it scared her.

"Oh, dear!" she cried. "It might be colic! An obstruction in her abdomen!"

Molly look concerned. "That can be

really serious!" she exclaimed. "Should we start back?"

Sarah shook her head. "I can't ride her like this. In fact, I don't think I should even walk her that far." She looked at Scarlet and then back at her friend. "Molly, you're Scarlet's only hope. You've got to get the vet, and fast! You've got to ride!"

A frightened look crossed Molly's face. "Me? Ride?" she said. "Is this some kind of joke?"

"This is no joke, Molly. You know what colic can do," Sarah said urgently. "Look at her."

Scarlet shuddered and groaned again. This time, however, the pain was too much to bear, and the horse's legs buckled beneath her. Sarah was right. If left untreated, colic could be deadly!

"Oh, Scarlet!" cried Sarah, as she ran to her on the ground. Scarlet lay on her side, wincing in pain.

Sarah started to panic. "She may even need an operation. Scarlet *has* to see a vet— now!" She burst out into tears. "Molly, please!" she begged in between sobs. "I'm so afraid for her!"

Molly looked at Sarah and Scarlet, and she knew what she had to do. She took a deep breath and put on her bravest face. "Okay, I'll go," Molly said. Then she looked at Calypso. "I mean *we'll* go."

Sarah momentarily stopped crying and looked up in relief. "You will? Oh, thank you!"

"Try not to worry," Molly said comfortingly. "It's going to be okay." Then she patted Calypso's flank. "Calypso and I will make sure of it."

Calypso neighed with approval. The horse was thrilled Molly was ready to ride again.

Molly paused before mounting Calypso. Then, finally conquering her fear, she hauled herself up into the saddle. Calypso was delighted to have Molly back in the saddle.

"Dr. Martin is due east from here," said Sarah, pointing.

"I know, Sarah. We'll get him," promised

60

Molly. "You can count on us."

Sarah wiped a tear from her eye. "I know we can," she said, as she watched Molly ride off across the pasture.

Sarah looked back at Scarlet. She hated to see her in so much pain and wondered if Molly would make it to the vet. And if the vet would make it out to the pasture in time!

CHAPTER 10

Sarah leaned over Scarlet and gave her a kiss on the nose. "Help's on the way, girl," she said to the ailing horse. She placed her hands at the base of Scarlet's ears and massaged them one at a time. "Does that feel good? This massage is supposed to keep you from going into shock."

Scarlet neighed appreciatively.

Next, with a flat hand, Sarah rubbed the horse's abdomen in a circular motion.

"That's it," Sarah said, relieved Scarlet was staying calm. "The vet's on the way."

Scarlet tossed her head, agitated. She gave a fearful whinny.

Sarah gasped. "Scarlet . . . are you afraid of the vet? There's nothing to be afraid of, girl," she reassured her. "It's going to be okay."

Secretly, Sarah tried to convince herself of that very fact as her face clouded with worry.

Meanwhile, Molly and Calypso galloped across the pasture, determined and unified in their mission to find the vet. Soon they came to the edge of a field. Molly tightened the reins, and they came to a stop. In front of them was a fence that stretched for miles in both directions.

"Well, girl," Molly said, patting Calypso's flank. "No sign of a gate." She took a deep breath. "I guess we don't have much of a choice, do we? We've got to face our fears."

Molly gazed ahead at the fence, trying to keep calm and focused. "We can do this. We can do this," she said. She remembered what

Will had taught in the jumping lesson. "Look straight ahead, heels down, lean forward, seat back . . ." With a tap of her heels, she urged Calypso forward and they cantered toward the fence.

The fence got closer and closer. . . .

Molly and Calypso looked more determined than ever. . . .

Calypso's front legs left the ground. . . .

And they cleared the fence perfectly!

"We did it, girl!" cheered Molly, as she reined Calypso in. "We really did it!"

Molly grinned and Calypso whinnied joyfully. Molly patted her horse affection-ately on the neck. They had done it together.

Then they headed off at a gallop to find the vet. There was no time to lose!

A little while later, Molly saw a large build-ing with a vet's sign out front. They had made it! Molly tethered Calypso to a hitching post near the entrance. Before going in, Molly gave her horse a grateful pat on the nose.

"Good job, girl. Thanks for the ride," she told the horse. "And thanks for bearing with me."

Calypso whinnied happily in return. She was so glad Molly had overcome this hurdle.

Back in the pasture, Sarah was doing her best to keep Scarlet steady and calm.

Suddenly, she heard the throb of an engine and looked up. A truck pulling a horse trailer was coming through the pasture.

"She did it! Molly did it!" cried Sarah, her face brightening. "Here comes the vet!"

The mention of the word *vet* made Scarlet nervous once again. She tossed her head back with anxiety.

"Shhh . . . Hush, now, Scarlet," said Sarah soothingly. She began rubbing the horse's ears again. "It's time for you to face *your* fears. Just like I told Molly. You can do it. You can let the vet help you."

Sarah stood up and waved to the approaching truck. She was so relieved to see it. Help had arrived at last!

CHAPTER
11

There was a lot going on inside the stable at Horseland. It had been quite an exciting day, for both the horses that competed *and* the ones that stayed behind. Shep was bringing everyone up to speed.

"...And then Molly and Calypso got the vet, and he brought Scarlet back here," he explained, his tail wagging. "You guys missed out on all the excitement!"

"*You're* the one who missed all the excitement, dog breath!" said Chili, tossing his head back arrogantly. Outside his stall hung a bright red ribbon. "We *ruled* at the competition! More ribbons for Horseland!" He neighed proudly.

Pepper stuck her head out of her stall and nodded in agreement. She had also earned a red ribbon at the competition.

"Well, *excuuuuse* me," replied Shep. "I guess winning a couple of colored ribbons is more important than Scarlet almost dying." He gave Chili and Pepper a stern look.

Just then Teeny approached Calypso's stall. She was bursting with energy and jumping up and down. "Oh, oh, oh! Calypso was really heroic! She saved Scarlet!" the little pig sang joyfully. "She was a hero! She saved her life!"

Calypso shook her head. "No, I didn't. The vet did," she said.

"Yes, but the vet wouldn't have gotten there in time if it hadn't been for you,"

Shep pointed out.

Calypso glanced over at Scarlet's stall. The Arabian horse looked so much better than she had before.

"Thank you, Calypso," Scarlet said gratefully. "I never should have tried to keep my pain a secret from everyone. All I did was suffer more, and I ended up having to see the vet anyway."

"Enough about Scarlet and Calypso!" complained Chili. He was jealous of them getting all the attention. "Did they win ribbons? No!"

Button piped up. "Will you give it a rest?" she said to Chili. "It's not like you took the first-place blue ribbon. Aztec did!"

"That's great!" said Calypso, impressed.

Scarlet looked at Aztec. "Why didn't you tell us?" she asked.

"It's not a big deal," Aztec replied bashfully. "If you ask me, Calypso and Molly are the heroes of the day."

All of the horses whinnied their agreement—except Chili and Pepper. After all, some things never change!

CHAPTER 12

The sun was setting over the distant mountains, casting a gorgeous red glow across Horseland. Everyone gathered at the fence railing thinking about what an eventful few days it had been. Some sat on the rail, and some just leaned while Sarah sat on a bale of hay, with Angora curled up by her feet and Teeny sitting next to her. Sarah was scratching Teeny behind the ears, and the pig was in heaven.

"I'm telling you, this girl was amazing!" Sarah said, as she beamed at Molly. "Thanks, Molly. You're the best."

Molly blushed. "Sarah, *you're* the one who helped me face my fear," she reminded her. "I know that I'll be frightened of other things, too, but maybe next time, I'll be able to handle it better."

"It's good to hear you sounding so positive again, Molly," Sarah told her.

Bailey and Alma agreed. They were impressed by Molly's strength and determination.

But Chloe and Zoey were not impressed at all.

"Very touching," said Zoey, rolling her eyes.

"I'm so touched, it makes me want to face one of *my* fears," Chloe said in a mocking tone.

Bailey and Alma looked at each other and shrugged dismissively. Molly rolled her eyes. They were used to Chloe acting like that.

On the ground, Teeny turned to see why Sarah had stopped scratching her. She stood on her hind legs and tried nudging Sarah with her front feet. When it didn't work, Teeny sat back on her haunches—and right on Angora's tail!

"Yeowl!" the cat cried out, jumping into the air.

The howl startled Chloe—so much so that she fell backward off the fence rail.

"Whoa!" she cried out, her arms waving wildly.

SPLASH! Chloe landed right in the water trough!

Everyone looked over to see what had happened. They couldn't believe it. Chloe was soaked!

"Hey, Chloe, was that one of your fears?" teased Alma.

The others laughed. Chloe, however, did not find it so funny—not one bit!

CHAPTER 13

A few days later, the riders are back in the arena, practicing their jumps. Molly and Calypso go first and successfully jump over a fence three poles high. The others applaud her.

"All right! You're getting better, Molly," Will says encouragingly.

"That was excellent!" agrees Sarah. "Great jump!"

"Bravo, Molly!" calls Alma.

Molly and Calypso both beam with pride. They have come a long way.

At the entrance to the arena, Shep, Teeny, and Angora watch the riders.

"Molly sure has learned how to jump, hasn't she?" Teeny says to the others.

Shep nods. "She's learned more than that," he adds. "Now she knows what to do when she's afraid."

"Oh, that's great!" cries Teeny. "Me too! Me too! From now on, I'm going to face *my* fears."

"Good thinking," Angora says to the pig. "So am I."

Teeny turns to Angora, astonished. "You mean you agree with something I said?" She can't believe her ears!

"Yep," says Angora. "Because the one thing I fear most is you stepping on my tail again! But as long as I face you, you can't do it!"

Angora's very pleased with her solution ...
until Jimber walks by and accidentally steps
on the cat's tail!

"*Yeowl!*" Angora cries, leaping into the
air again.

"Ouch!" says Shep. "Looks like you're

going to have to face both ways at once, right, Angora?"

Angora glares at Shep. "Very funny," she says.

It looks like Angora will have to come up with another plan to face her fears. Perhaps Molly can give her some pointers!

Meet the Riders and Their Horses

Sarah Whitney is a natural when it comes to horses. Sarah's horse, **Scarlet**, is a black Arabian mare.

Alma Rodriquez is confident and hard-working. Alma's horse, **Button**, is a skewbald pinto mare.

Molly Washington
has a great sense of
humor and doesn't
take anything
seriously—except her
riding. Molly's horse,
Calypso, is a spotted
Appaloosa mare.

Chloe Stilton
is often forceful and
very competitive, even
when it comes to her
sister, Zoey. Chloe's
horse, **Chili**, is a gray
Dutch Warmblood
stallion.

Zoey Stilton
is Chloe's sister. She's
also very competitive
and spoiled.
Zoey's horse, **Pepper**,
is a gray Dutch
Warmblood mare.

Bailey Handler
likes to take chances.
His parents own
Horseland Ranch.
Bailey's horse, **Aztec**,
is a Kiger mustang.

Will Taggert is Bailey's cousin and has lived with the family since he was little. Because he's the oldest, Will is in charge when the adults aren't around. Will's horse, **Jimber**, is a palomino stallion.

Spotlight on Calypso

Breed: Spotted Appaloosa

Physical characteristics:
- Broad body
- Thick bones
- Colorful spotted coat
- Strong durable hooves

Personality:
- Intelligent
- Willing
- Gentle
- Versatile

Fun facts:
- Ancient cave drawings from as far back as 20,000 years depict horses with spotted coats.
- No two Appaloosa coats are exactly the same.
- The Appaloosa is the state horse of Idaho.

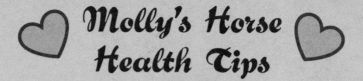

Molly's Horse Health Tips

It's important to keep your horse healthy. Here are some things you should do for your horse regularly.

- ♞ Your horse should be vaccinated and dewormed by a veterinarian regularly.
- ♞ Your horse's teeth should be checked once a year by a veterinarian.

- Check your horse every day for indications of illness or injury:
  - Eyes: They should be fully open with no discharge.
  - Legs: Look for any swelling or cuts that may need treatment.
  - Hooves: Check for cracks or a bad smell.
  - Coat: It should look sleek.
  - Stomach: They should have a healthy appetite.

Some common horse illnesses are colic and laminitis.

COLIC

Changes in feed, gas buildup, or parasites can cause stomach or abdominal pain for your horse. Colic can be fatal if not treated in time.

Call the veterinarian immediately if you notice any of these symptoms in your horse:
- Sweating
- Dullness of the coat
- Loss of appetite
- Restlessness
- The horse frequently looks at its belly or flank.

LAMINITIS

Overfeeding of rich, lush grass or prolonged work on hard ground can cause this painful hoof condition. It is more common in ponies.

Call the veterinarian immediately if you notice any of these symptoms in your horse:

- ♞ An increased pulse in the horse's lower limb
- ♞ The horse refuses to walk or stand up.
- ♞ The horse puts more weight on the back hooves (laminitis often affects the front hooves).